A Gift to Remember

A Gift to Remember
A Pocket Rocket Christmas Novella

By Cyan Tayse

Other books by Cyan Tayse

Pocket Rocket Novellas

Have you Ever…?
Blank Canvas
A Gift to Remember

Brief Encounters Novellas

Thick as Thieves

Chapter One

Dan

"I still don't get why our Christmas do is at an art gallery." Ethan grabs a glass from a passing waiter, taking a large mouthful. "I mean, we're hardly a refined bunch." He leans in, speaking out the side of his mouth. "I heard it's 'cause the boss man's got a thing for the one organising this shindig." He waves his hands in the air, as if caressing the female form. "Anything for a bit of action."

"I don't know, I think it's kinda cool. Something a bit different." My eyes travel over the image in front of me. "And you have to admit, the model is pretty hot."

Ethan turns to see what's caught my eye and lets out a whistle. "I certainly wouldn't kick her out of bed, that's for damn sure." His gaze rakes over the nude figure. "Not unless I was finishing her on the floor." He snorts, tossing the rest of the wine down his throat with a grimace. "Who serves wine to athletes? Don't they know we're beer drinkers through and through?"

"Geez, you don't have much to complain about, do you?" Cara sidles up in her red, velour Santa dress that leaves little to the imagination. I can't help but drink her in. With her long, luscious legs and perky breasts playing peekaboo over the top of her dress, she's a knockout.

"Well, if it isn't the Blonde Bullet herself." Ethan smirks, slinging an arm around her shoulders and pulling her in for a hug. "Trust you to try and show up the artist's work." His eyes skim over her body appreciatively, and I have to restrain the growl that wants to come out. What we had was one epic night of lust, nothing more. But damn if I wouldn't like another crack at it.

Cara plants a kiss on his cheek with a chuckle. "Oh, you charmer, you." Turning to me, she winks. "How goes it, Dan the man?" She peers around the room. "What? No entourage? No girl on your arm?" Then in an exaggerated whisper behind her hand to Ethan, she says, "He never got over me, did he?" Her tongue darts out in a playful gesture, but all I can think of is having it wrapped around my cock. This woman will be the death of me.

It's been almost two months since that night at the flat. Two long, lonely months of wet dreams and taking matters into my own hands. A sad existence if ever there was one. Long gone are the days of Dan Knight, playboy extraordinaire. Now I'm a pathetic shell of a man, pining after something I can never have again.

"Nah. You ruined him for all eternity, I'm afraid." He holds his finger up, letting it bend sadly before bursting into hysterics.

I slap a hand to his chest. "Yeah, because you've got so much going on with the ladies, right?" I glance around the room. "Practically batting them away with a stick, eh bro?"

He punches my arm, muttering, "dick" under his breath.

I turn my attention back to Cara. "How've you been?"

"Oh, you know." She waves a hand through the air. "More pussy than I can handle."

Ethan chokes on his drink, almost spitting it across the room.

Cara laughs, shaking her head. "You really missed out on that one, Ethan. Bri sure is a little firecracker in the sack!"

"Cara!" Bri appears from the crowd behind. "I'm sure they don't want to hear that."

"Hear about two hot chicks making out? I think Ethan's died and gone to heaven." She swats Bri on the ass, making her laugh.

"Stop!" She straightens her dress and dips her head down, talking through her hair. "Hi, Ethan."

His cheeks redden as he clears his throat, offering a small wave. "Hey, Bri."

Cara's eyes flick between the two of them before saying, "Awkward," in a singsongy voice. "You two need a minute?"

Since that night, Ethan had refused to come over unless Bri wasn't there. He was too embarrassed that she'd chosen a chick over his dick. Of course, I never let him live it down either.

"Nah, we're good." Ethan grabs another passing glass and raises it in the air. "You look good, Bri."

"Thanks, so do you." She leans in to Cara, and they exchange a look before Cara shakes her head. They seem to hold a silent conversation with just their eyes.

"Right." Cara slaps her hands on her thighs. "I guess we'd better get back to it. These drinks won't hand themselves out."

"You're waitressing?" I ask with a raised brow as I look her up and down once more. "In that?"

Cara looks down at her dress. "What? You don't like my slutty Mrs Claus outfit?" She pouts.

"I didn't say that. I just thought maybe you were… um." I stop, glancing at Bri.

"Oh, you thought I was cheating on my girlfriend with one of these schmucks?" She waves her hand around the room with a tsk. "Danny, Danny, Danny. You should know better than that." She pulls Bri in to her side, twirling a strand of her red hair around a finger. "Once you go red, you get lots of head." She winks.

"Uh, I don't think that's—"

"To-may-toe, to-mah-toe. You get what I'm saying. Or do I need to spell it out for you?" She flits her eyes back and forth between us. "She's got a tongue like a serpent and knows how to use it."

"Oh God." Bri buries her head in Cara's shoulder. "Please stop."

"Don't be embarrassed, baby. Half these jocks probably don't even know where to find the clit, let alone the G-spot." She waggles her eyebrows suggestively. "She could teach you a thing or two, I'm sure."

"Ooh, burn!" Ethan brings his fist to his mouth as he chuckles, turning to look at me.

"I don't recall hearing any complaints." I take another sip of the dry wine, raising one eyebrow at her.

"A lady doesn't talk with her mouth full. That would be considered rude." She winks before throwing her head back and laughing.

Bri reaches out, placing a hand on my arm. "Ignore her. I'm sure you were great." She gives Cara that same look again, and she acquiesces with a roll of her eyes.

"All right, fine." She throws her hands in the air and tips her head to the side as she lets out a sigh and says, "You're a great lay, Danny boy." Then she meets Bri's eye again. "Happy now?"

Bri nods, grabbing her hand. "Come on, we should get back to the kitchen." With a wave over her shoulder and a sway to her hips,

Cara follows behind Bri as they push through the crowd. I don't miss the heads turning as she passes. That girl could make even a blind man drool.

"You're dreaming, mate." Ethan slaps a hand on my shoulder, drawing my attention away from her ass. "You had your one night with the both of them. It's not gonna happen again. Lightning doesn't strike twice."

I shrug his hand off, snatching another drink from a passing tray. I know he's right, but that doesn't mean I have to be happy about it. The image of Cara and Bri in the kitchen that night is still fresh in my mind, and it was the hottest damn thing I've ever seen. You can't blame a man for hoping for a second shot.

Chapter Two

Hailee

"Are you sure I look okay?" Aroha brushes a hand down the front of her dress, twisting and turning in front of the mirror. "I feel like my butt looks big."

"Your butt looks as gorgeous as ever. Now go." I swat her behind, ushering her towards the door. "We can't be late to our own party."

"Can we really call it that? A bunch of rugby heads all gawking at my curves doesn't sound like my idea of a party." She grabs her purse, slinging it over her shoulder.

"Admit it, you love the attention." I plant a soft kiss on her lips.

"I love *your* attention." She runs a hand down the side of my face, gently cupping my cheek. "The rest I can take or leave." Her eyes pierce through to my soul and I feel my cheeks redden with the intensity. Even after all these months, she still has the power to bring me to my knees with just a look. Heat rushes straight to my core, and part of me wonders if we have enough time to slip out the back before we meet the crowds.

"Knock, knock." Angelique steps through the door. "Are you ready?" Her hair is piled on top of her head with wisps floating about her face as per usual. Her floating skirts have been replaced by a long, fitted dress with bell sleeves in a beautiful red brocade, and in place of boots, she wears low heels to match.

"Wow. You look amazing, Angelique." I take hold of her shoulders and kiss each cheek. She blushes, waving a hand through the air.

"Oh hush." She smooths a hand down the front of her dress. "I feel so awkward in this get up."

"Well, you shouldn't. You're a fox!" Aroha pulls her in for a hug. "At least now the eyes won't all be on my ass." She winks over her shoulder.

Angelique chuckles. "I think they'll be on more than just your rear end." She smiles warmly, placing a hand on my arm. "There's a lot of talk going around the room, and it's all good. They love you." She turns to look at Aroha. "Both of you."

"You're a star, baby." Aroha brushes her lips against mine. "Just like I knew you would be."

"It's you they're looking at." I smile, ducking my head.

With her finger, she lifts my chin to meet her gaze. "It's *you* who made them see me." Her eyes glisten with joy and love, sending shivers through my body. Sometimes I feel as though my heart could burst with the power of our love.

"This is a big night for both of you. The launch of your careers." She takes my hand. "You should be so proud of yourself, Hailee. From the moment I saw your work I could see an immense talent, but over the last few months you've grown, and your passion shines through your art." She stops, swiping a hand under her eye and giving her head a shake to clear the tears. "You've surpassed anything I can teach you now, and I can't wait to see what you bring to the world. Because as long as you're in it, I know there will be beauty."

My hand flies to my chest as I take in her words. "Thank you," I whisper, fighting back the tears that want to break free. "Thank you for believing in me and helping me get here." I wave my hand around the room. "Having my work displayed in the Christchurch Art Gallery is something I've dreamed of my whole life." I shake my head, bringing a hand to my face. "I still can't believe it's actually happening."

"Well, believe it, baby, because we're here, and they're going to love you as much as I do." Aroha grips the door handle, turning to grasp my hand. "Your adoring fans await, my love." She pushes through the entrance, and my heart leaps into my throat as I see the face of my muse beaming back at me from the wall opposite. Even in my paintings she manages to steal my breath and set my heart racing. Every inch of her is on display around the room; from the tribal artwork across her back, to the brilliant emerald of her eyes and the ebony strands of her hair, she adorns the walls and foyer for all to see. My chest fills with pride as I witness the stares of onlookers. They see it too, the beauty that radiates from within.

"This way." Angelique ushers me to the podium in the centre of the room. This is it. The moment when I become more than just a name on a painting. I become the artist.

Chapter Three

Cara

"Taunting him isn't going to make this any easier, you know," Bri admonishes as she pulls the apron over her head. "We need him to be in a good mood."

"Stop worrying so much, sweetcheeks. Before the night is through, I'll have him in the palm of my hand."

"Oh, will you now?" She quirks an eyebrow at me, folding her arms across her chest. The action makes her creamy breasts push against the bodice of her dress, and my eyes instantly drop to those ample mounds. "And where will I be while he's in your hands?"

My tongue runs across my bottom lip as I picture what I want to do to her right now. "Preferably on my face, but I'm easy, you should know that." I grin, lifting my eyes away from the goods. "I'll take you any which way you want. In fact—" I look over my shoulder towards the back entrance. "We can always sneak out there for a quickie up against the fence." I waggle my eyebrows at her. "You game?"

That gorgeous shade of pink colours her cheeks as she ducks her head with a smirk. It's so easy to get her worked up.

I grab her hips and pull her in close, arching my back so I can see her face. "Come on. There are plenty of servers here, they won't miss us." Brushing a loose strand of hair behind her ear, I lean in close and whisper, "I'll do that thing you like." Her sharp inhalation of breath has me grinning like the cat who got the cream. Without giving her a chance to turn me down, I grab her hand and lead her out the back. A nervous giggle bubbles up from her chest, and she quickly covers her mouth with a hand, peering behind us. "Don't worry, no one saw us." I pull her down to the darkened corner and spin on my heels, pinning her against the cool brick wall.

"Oh," slips from her lips before I run my tongue along her jawline and up to the sweet spot under her ear.

"I'll have that pussy purring in no time," I whisper, and she shivers in anticipation. Taking hold of her hands, I bring them up above her head, pressing them into the brickwork. "Now, don't move a muscle."

"Mmhmm," she hums, nodding her head in agreeance. We've played this game many a time, but never in a public place. The thrill of being caught heightens my arousal, and I can tell by the flush of her cheeks, Bri is feeling it too.

With my hands running slowly down the curves of her body, I drop to my knees, lifting the red velour above my head. Her giggle is quickly replaced with a moan as I run my nose across the edge of her panties. Pushing the silky fabric aside, I flatten my tongue and lick from opening to clit in one fluid motion. Her hips jerk towards my face, and I pull back. "Uh-uh-uh, Bri. I said don't move."

She whimpers, but holds still, waiting.

"Good girl." I dive in again, lapping at her soft folds while my hands work her ass. I know we don't have much time before they start looking for us, so I increase the pressure, my tongue now circling her swollen bud.

"Oh, God," she hisses under her breath, and I can tell how much she wants to move by the shake of her thighs. It's taking everything in her to stop from bucking under my tongue. I need to kick it up a notch.

Curling my hand around the back of her thigh, I draw a finger through her folds and back towards her ass. She's so wet, I leave a trail behind me and use it to circle her puckered entrance. A low moan escapes her lips as I pull her clit between my teeth and delve a finger inside her.

"Oh, fuck me, Cara... I can't... I have to..." she pants, her body practically vibrating with need.

"Come for me, baby," I coo, flicking my tongue even faster. "Come on my lips." My finger presses further into her ass, just enough to send her over the edge.

"Oh, God, yes!" she cries out, grabbing hold of my head as she rides her ecstasy over my face. I'm not even mad that she moved; just means I get to punish that sweet pussy again later.

"Hey, you!" a voice calls from down the alley.

"Shit!" Bri hisses, pushing the skirt of her dress back down over her thighs.

"What are you doing back there?" The man steps out into the night, the hustle and bustle of the kitchen now echoing down the alley.

I casually get to my feet and swipe a hand across my mouth. "Just having a snack break, boss. Be right there!"

"You're being paid to work not skive off. It's only a four-hour shift."

"Yes, boss." I salute like a soldier and march my way back to the door while Bri hides in the shadows. "Won't happen again."

"Better bloody not." He pushes through the door, letting it fall shut behind me.

"Speeches are about to start, and there are men out there without drinks." He shoves a bottle of wine in each of my hands and points me towards the counter laden with trays and glasses. "Get to work."

Chapter Four

Aroha

As per usual, Hailee steals my breath away as she steps up to the podium. I can tell she's nervous by the way her eyes dart around the room. Lifting my hand, I give a little wave so she can find me, and as soon as her eyes meet mine, her shoulders loosen and she takes a breath.

"Th-thank you all for coming tonight." She smiles, and it lights up the room. "This has been a dream of mine for as long as I can remember, and I'd like to thank the Christchurch Art Gallery for taking a chance on me and displaying my work for you tonight." She turns her gaze back to Angelique.

"And thank you to my mentor, Angelique, for helping my dreams come true." She smiles, raising a glass in the air. Angelique steeples her hands and brings them to her chest with a nod. "You will have noticed that many of my pieces are focused on one model alone. My muse." She finds my eyes again. Curling a finger in the air, she beckons me to come forward. "This is Aroha, the inspiration behind this collection." She takes my hand, bringing me to stand beside her. "Without her, I don't think I would be standing here today. She helped me find my light." Her hand squeezes mine. "And on that note, I believe it's time to light the tree."

A burly man with kind eyes steps up to the podium. "Thank you, Hailee. It was kind of you to share this night with the Nomads." He turns to the crowd. "Boys, it's been a cracker year. You've put in the hard yards and it's paid off."

"Nomads are number one!" someone shouts from the crowd.

"Damn straight. And we'll stay number one if you keep working together like you have been." He takes a mouthful of his drink before continuing. "Now, let's get this tree lit." He pauses, eyeing the crowd. "And that better be all that gets lit tonight, understand? I'm talking to you, Ethan."

"Aww shit, coach. It was one time."

"Yeah yeah. Try to be civilised, all right? We're in the presence of ladies." He nods his head towards Angelique with a grin. It's not hard to see what he's hoping for later. A bit of how's your father in the back alley, no doubt. And good luck to him. After everything she's done for Hailee, she deserves to get a bit of loving.

"Would you help me?" Hailee asks, pulling my hand towards the tree.

"Anything for you." Her cheeks redden as she ducks her chin. I don't think I'll ever tire of seeing her reaction to me. She may have found her light, but she still hasn't quite found all her confidence, and I'll spend every minute of every day trying to bring it out in her, for the rest of our lives if I have to. But for now, I'll enjoy the way her face flushes when I meet her gaze, and how her heart races when our skin meets.

"Here it is." Her words are breathless as she stops in front of the tree. With shaking hands, she grasps two plugs from beneath and hands one to me. "This is for you," she whispers.

I hadn't noticed until it was right in front of me, that it's not actually a tree, but another piece of art. My eyes land first on the pyramid of images piled atop each other to resemble a tree. There must be hundreds of them, all fanned out to make the branches. Snapshots of our life together. "This is…" I stare, unable to find words. "How did you…" My hand flies to my mouth as I spy the star on top. It's made up of korus, like my tattoos. "Hailee," I whisper as my eyes fill with tears. "It's beautiful."

"Not as beautiful as you." She nods at the plug in my hand. "Ready?"

I hold the plug out towards her, waiting for hers to join mine. Her hand rests on mine as the tree lights up behind us, but I can't take my eyes away from her. She's the most amazing person I've ever met, and she keeps surprising me.

"Are you going to look at it?" she asks with a smile.

I peel my eyes away from hers slowly and take in the tiny lanterns adorning the tree. They draw my attention to the ornaments I'd missed. The first, a tiny chaise lounge like the one I'd posed on in Angelique's class. A giggle slips out as my fingers caress the piece of furniture. Next, my eyes are drawn to a miniature Bonnie Tyler album, and I'm instantly transported back to when I first picked her up – *Total Eclipse of the Heart* was on full volume. Enjoying this little game, I quickly scan for the next one; a palette, much like the one she'd been using when she painted me for the first time.

She's put so much thought into this, and I'm sure no one else gets the significance of each piece like I do, but right now, as I find each ornament attached to our lives together, it feels as though we're the only two people in the room.

The lights lead me further around the tree to the last ornament. This one is different to the others. It's not an ornament, but a heart shaped box. My eyes search out Hailee, but she's not there.

"You have my heart, Aroha," she whispers from behind me. "Open it."

With shaking hands, I reach out for the small velveteen box and pry it open. A gasp slips from my lips as I stare at the beautiful jade necklace shaped in an eternal twist, signifying the joining of two people for eternity.

Two delicate hands wrap around mine. "Aroha, you took my broken pieces and made them whole again. You showed me that even through pain, there is beauty, and sometimes you have to go through the hurt, to find the thing most precious to you." Dropping to one knee, she pulls another heart shaped box from her purse. Inside is a rose gold band made of three threads twisted together in a braid. "Aroha, I wish I could put on canvas the light you have inside for all to see, because it truly is a thing of beauty. And I'd like to spend all eternity trying to find the beauty of the world with you by my side." She swipes a tear from her eye and smiles up at me. "Please, will you marry me?"

Tears of pure joy cascade down my cheeks. This beautiful woman who is not fond of the limelight, just proposed to me in front of a room full of strangers. I was wrong, she *has* found her confidence, tenfold it would seem.

Dropping to my knees in front of her, I nod my head, yes. "Of course I'll marry you." She takes hold of my finger and slips the ring on. I hold it up for all to see. "You see that? She put a ring on it! That means she likes me."

Cheers and laughter rumble around the room, but it's Hailee I'm focused on. Taking her face in my hands, I bring her lips to mine. "You are the most amazing woman I've ever met," I whisper before sealing our lips. "This is the best Christmas present I've ever had."

Chapter Five

Dan

"Seriously? She's a carpet muncher too? I can't catch a break!" Ethan throws his hands in the air.

"Yeah, because you had a shot with her in the first place," I joke, helping myself to a salmon and cream cheese breadstick. "You didn't even say boo as she walked passed you."

"Oh, 'cause you're having so much luck with the ladies? At least I'm looking. You've given up." He shakes his head. "Dan Knight, pussy whipped by two broads who won't give him the time of day."

"I'm not pussy whipped," I scoff. "I could get laid if I wanted to." I shrug my shoulders, looking around the room. "Just haven't seen anyone worth pursuing is all."

"Shit, man, you lose your eyesight as well as your balls? There's plenty of women sniffing around, waiting for a taste of Knight." He slaps his hand down on my shoulder. "It's a sad state of affairs when you're too blind to see what's right in front of you, offered up on a silver bloody platter."

I don't know what he's talking about. There are no women banging on my door. At least, not that I know of.

Pussy whipped. I'll show him pussy whipped.

"I'd love to see this platter you're on about. Point me in the right direction and I'll gladly take my pick," I say. "In fact, you can choose for me. How's that for pussy whipped?"

Ethan throws his head back, laughing boisterously. "You asking me to be your wingman? Since when do you need help in that area?"

"I don't. Like I said, I can get laid anytime I want."

"Right. You *chose* to have a dry couple of months, then." He brings both hands up to point at me with a wink. "Gotcha."

"You know, you can be a real ass sometimes."

"Someone's gotta keep you on your toes. Ain't no woman to do it for you." He smirks, dodging away from my fist.

"Ooh, someone likes it rough." Cara sidles up beside me with a tray full of drinks. "Nothing like a bit of foreplay to get the juices flowing." She waves the tray under our noses. "Speaking of juices… how's about a little something wet?" Her tongue darts out to lap at her plump lips, and I can't help but follow with my eyes.

Jesus, this woman. I swear she's been put on this earth to torment me and every other red-blooded male out there with her teasing.

Huh. Perhaps Ethan is right. I *am* pussy whipped, and I don't even get the pussy at the end of it. It's just dangled in front of me, taunting me, reminding me of what I'm missing out on. Meanwhile, she's out getting hers, and I'm left with my dick in my hands, imagining it's her instead. *Fuck, I'm pathetic.*

"I'd like a taste." Ethan hooks his thumb over his shoulder towards me. "But he'd like a second helping." He shrugs. "Bros before hoes, ya know?" Then he walks away, chuckling to himself.

Dick.

Cara's brow hitches as she turns to me with a smirk. "Is that so?"

"Uh… I mean…" I rake a hand through my hair, giving in. "Yeah. Yes. I'm a man. What do you expect?"

She purses her lips, pointing a finger at her chest. "With just me? Because, I'm a package deal now." She winks. "No one goes near this bad boy—" she makes a V shape with her hands, pointing towards her crotch, "—without Bri's say so."

Fuck, is she for real?

"And if she says yes?"

"Then it's on like Donkey Kong." She flicks her hair over her shoulder and sashays away.

Chapter Six

Bri

"Well?" I grab her arm and lead her out to the kitchen with me. "What did he say?"

"I didn't really get around to that part yet. Thought maybe we could sweeten the deal a little first?" She waggles her eyebrows at me. "Dude's got the bluest balls. I think he might explode if we don't help him out."

"Oh, so it's a civil service kind of a thing? Doing it for the good of the country?" I fold my arms across my chest and jut out my hip. Her eyes fall straight to my breasts, as I knew they would.

"Mmhmm. Definitely for the good of the country and not just a pity fuck." She licks her lips as I press my chest out further. The way she devours me with her eyes is such a turn on, and as long as she keeps looking at me like that, we can do whatever she wants.

"Well, if it's for the good of the country, then it'd be wrong not to do it." I grin as her eyes flick up to meet mine.

"Yeah?"

I shrug. "Sure. I'm the one who gets to go home with you, right?"

"Always."

"Then, let's do this thang." I bop on my hip and snap my fingers. Cara laughs, leaning in to kiss my nose.

"Ah, my little Fifty Cents. You're so gangsta."

"Fifty Cents? We are officially the whitest couple on the planet."

Cara slices a hand through the air until it lands on her stomach. "Girl, you crazy. I think I wanna have your baby," she sings, wiggling her hips to an imaginary beat. "Wo-man, wo-man, wo-man, what a mighty wo-man. Yes she is!"

Giggling, I pull her hands into mine to get her to stop. "You'll get us in trouble again."

"Us?" Her lips form a perfect pout. "I think you'll find I took the fall while you were still coming down from your mind-blowing O." Cocking her head to the side, she adds, "You're welcome, by the way."

"These trays won't serve themselves, ladies." Walter storms past us, a tray in each arm. "Chop chop."

Cara stands to attention, doing a one-fingered salute behind his back. "Yes, drill sergeant, sir!"

"Come on, we'd better get back out there." I load my tray with more breadsticks and canapes. "We can't afford to lose this gig."

"Pfft. There are plenty of ways to make cash. Don't you worry your pretty little head." She runs a hand down my hair to the side of my face. "Let Mama look after you."

Chapter Seven

Hailee

She said yes!

My muse, my girl and now, my fiancée. I was so scared she'd think it was all too soon, but if I've learned anything from being with Aroha, it's that you have to embrace the fear and pain and do it anyway. You can't let fear hold you back from what you truly want, and what I truly want, is Aroha. The woman who lives up to her name; love and compassion. She is aroha personified.

With her arm wrapped firmly around my waist, we make our way around the room, chatting with various groups about my paintings, our process, and of course, my proposal. Up until we stepped through the door into the gallery, I wasn't sure if I'd be able to go through with it, but when I saw her face so full of pride as I gave my speech, I knew I had to do it. She deserves that and so much more. Hell, I'd give her the world if I could, but hopefully my love and devotion is enough.

"Simply stunning," a woman gushes to her partner. "I love the way the light falls on her hair, giving her an angelic appeal."

"Let me guess, you want it?" The man beams down at her, and my fingers itch to sketch the adoring look in his eyes.

"Am I that obvious?" She chuckles, reaching up to caress his stubbled cheek.

"You? Obvious? Never," he laughs, reaching for his cheque book. "How much for this one?" he asks, pointing at one of my favourite images. It was from our first session together, when she not only bared her skin to me, but her soul too. I had thought the exact same thing then; she looked like an angel.

"One million dollars," Aroha pipes up with her pinky finger held to the corner of her mouth.

The man doesn't miss a beat, tipping his head back to laugh.

"No, really. It's one million dollars," she says with a serious tone. "We have a wedding to save for."

I can't help but laugh. "No, it's not that much, honestly. If you head up to the front, they're taking payments up there." I point him in the direction of the foyer before turning to Aroha with a hand on my hip. "You can't go upping my prices before I've even made my first sale."

"Hey, your paintings are worth every damn cent of that million. I mean, look at that face." She holds her arms under the painting like a game show hostess presenting a prize. "Who wouldn't pay a million dollars for that face on their wall?"

"For a million smackers that face had better be doing more than just sitting on my wall." A perky blonde in a Mrs Claus suit holds a tray of drinks out towards us. "I mean, a pretty face on a wall is one thing, but a pretty face going to town on the V train? Now *that's* worth a million bucks." She winks, swinging her hips as she walks over to the next group. "Something moist for your lips?"

"Tell me she didn't just say that to the head of the Society of Arts," I groan, bringing my hand up to rub my temple.

"Oh, you mean the well-to-do stiff over there? Yeah, she did." Aroha smirks, lifting her glass to her lips. "If it's any consolation, it looks as though he enjoyed it."

Chapter Eight

Cara

"What's the deal with that chick?" Ethan nods his head towards a tall drink of water standing by herself in the corner. "She bat for your team or what?"

"Hmm, hard to say. My gaydar isn't picking anything up from her, but I reckon I could turn her." I wink, turning on my heels and strutting towards her before Ethan grabs my arm, pulling me back.

"No! Keep your mitts to yourself. You already stole one girl from me. Let me have this one."

"Aww, is someone feeling left out? You want a cuddle?" I open my arms out wide. "Will that make you feel better?"

"You know, it really might." He shuffles into my embrace, his arms wrapping tightly around my middle with a sigh. "Is it too much to ask that there be one straight girl who's into me?"

"Aww, there there." I stroke a hand down the back of his head like I would a baby. "I'm sure you'll find the woman of your wet dreams."

"Huh, I already found her." He pulls back. "She ended up shagging my best mate and hers."

"What can I say? The ladies find me irresistible."

He snorts. "Just the ladies, huh?"

"Well, maybe the men too." I flick my hair. "It's my raw, animal magnetism. Here." I pull him back into me and shimmy up and down his body. "Let me rub some of my magnetism onto you."

"Uh, thanks?"

"Now, go get 'er, Tiger." I slap his ass and send him on his way.

"Do I even want to know what that was about?" Bri inches up beside me.

"Ethan's on the prowl." I swipe a hand under my eye as I watch him saunter towards the corner. "They grow up so fast."

"Aww, I hope he gets her. He's such a sweet guy."

"Speaking of sweet guys, how about we go play hide the lollipop with Dan?" Bri laughs as I press my tongue to the inside of my cheek in the universal sign for a blow job.

"You really think this will work?"

"Do I think sticking his dick in my mouth will butter him up for what we have to tell him? Uh, yeah, I do. Do I need to remind you what this mouth did to you earlier?" Her cheeks flush as she shakes her head. "Damn right. This mouth can work magic."

"I know it can, but this is... It's a big deal."

"What's a big deal?" Dan sneaks in between the two of us. "You talking about me again?"

"Oh, of course. We never *stop* talking about you." Pressing my chest against his, I bat my lashes. "Dan, the big deal, Knight."

"I… uh…" He blinks, stuttering over his words as he watches my lips. "What?"

"Whatsa matter, Dan? You lost for words?" I grin, leaning in to whisper in his ear. "That's okay, you don't need words for what we have in mind." His Adam's apple bobs as he swallows, and his tongue darts out to wet his lips. "We've got a present for you, Danny boy. I even wrapped it with a bow." Taking his hand, I lead him to where Bri waits.

"Quickly, before Walter sees," she whispers, ushering us down a corridor.

"Where are we going?" Dan asks, finding his tongue.

"Just down here." The sounds of the party fade into the background the further we go into the gallery. Bri leads us around the corner, through a row of tall sunflowers and into a room filled with yellow. A moon made of cheese hangs from the ceiling, and an array of cushions fill a pit in the centre of the room.

"This is art? Shit, even I could do this."

"I know, right? We're in the wrong business." Bri places her hands on her hips, looking around the room. "I don't really get what it's meant to be, but it looks soft so…"

"It's golden." I slip my hands around her waist and tug on the ribbons holding her dress together until they come loose in my hands. "I love unwrapping presents, don't you?" When I step away, her dress falls to the floor and she's left standing in her white lace panties and bra. Dan hasn't moved from his spot, but his eyes follow my every move.

Walking behind Bri, I brush her hair to one side and lick a trail up her neck to her ear. She lets out a sigh, leaning her head back to rest on my shoulder. My hands trace the curves of her hips as I slide my fingers under the lace of her panties and start to push down. Dropping to my knees, I follow her form with my lips as I help her out of her panties and toss them aside.

"Fuck," Dan hisses between his teeth, but still doesn't move.

"Whatsa matter? You waiting for an invite?" On all fours, I crawl towards him, stopping at his feet. "Need a little help getting out of those pants, sailor?" Running my hands up his strong thighs, I place a kiss to the bulge at the front of his pants before unzipping him and pulling the material down. His cock springs free, and I run the flat of my tongue from base to tip before wrapping my lips around him with a hum. His hands fall to my head, gripping my hair in his fists as he throws his head back.

"Fuck, your mouth feels good."

Bri takes hold of my chin and pulls my lips to hers, while her hand takes over pumping his cock. My hands roam her body, landing between her thighs. A whimper falls from her lips as I slide my fingers through her wet folds and up to circle her clit.

No longer standing by the side, Dan sinks to his knees, his hands pulling at the soft fabric of my dress until I'm bare.

"No underwear?" He quirks a brow. "So fucking hot."

"Underwear is overrated." I wink, nodding towards my freshly waxed pussy. "You like your present?"

His fingers trace the bow of hair, and the corner of his lips lift into a grin. "Full of surprises, aren't you?"

"You don't know the half of it, baby." I thrust my hips up. "Go ahead and open your present." Rolling to my back, I spread my legs. "I've got my own present to unwrap." Bri straddles my chest, her glistening pussy as enticing as ever. Sliding my hands up her stomach, I cup her soft mounds, gently kneading as I run my tongue in lazy circles around her tightened nub.

"Oh yeah," she sighs, grinding her pussy on my face. "Just like that."

Dan groans from behind, his hands pressing my thighs wider as his tongue laps at my soft flesh. A thick finger pushes inside, curling up and hitting that sweet spot until I can't help but buck against his face. Breaking away from Bri, I cry out, "Fuck yes!" His hands clamp around my thighs, holding me in place while I ride out my orgasm. I slap a hand to Bri's ass. "Turn around." She does as she's told, spinning around until her ass is in my face.

Dan brings my legs up to rest on his shoulders as he lines his cock up to my entrance. He takes Bri's lips with his own as he slowly pushes his cock to the hilt.

Using both hands, I palm her cheeks, spreading her wide and lapping at her puckered entrance. With my thumb, I follow my tongue, rubbing circles and pressing ever so gently. She whimpers, arching her back and pushing her ass onto my mouth. Her hand trails down to tease her clit as I increase the pressure with my tongue. I can feel my own pleasure spiraling to a crescendo as Dan pounds into me with wild abandon.

"Oh fuck!" Bri cries out as her body begins to shudder and pulse with her release. She stills her body, letting me take her over the edge like only I can.

Dan picks up the pace, his thighs slapping against my flushed skin as he races to the finish. With one final thrust, he roars, throwing his head back.

I wait for his panting and mine to subside before asking, "How're those blue balls feeling now?"

He barks out a laugh. "Much better, thanks."

"Hey, if you can't rely on your friends to help you out of a bind, who can you rely on?" I sink my teeth into the soft flesh in front of me. "Isn't that right, Bri?"

"Mmhmm. That's what friends are for."

"I mean, I'd even go so far as to say we're like family. Wouldn't you, Bri?"

She nods, swinging her leg over and climbing off my face. "Definitely family."

"Ah, okay." Dan reaches a hand up to scratch the back of his neck. "I'm not sure I follow."

"Well." I reach out and take hold of Bri's hand. "As fun as that was, it's not the only present we have for you."

Chapter Nine

Aroha

"Have you seen Angelique anywhere?" Hailee asks, a look of concern on her face.

"Mmhmm. She's over there." I tip my glass in the direction of the foyer. "With that stocky bloke. I swear it's the third guy I've seen give it a crack." I laugh with a shake of my head. "Quite the popular lady."

"Can you blame them? She looks stunning in that dress." Hailee watches Angelique with affection. More than just a mentor, she's become a friend to us both. It's nice to see her smiling and having fun.

"Now now, do I have to wave my ring under your nose and remind you that you are now a kept woman?"

She places a hand to her chest. "I'm the kept woman? Pretty sure I'm the one who put a ring on it."

"You make a valid point. I guess we'll see who's keeping who when this shindig is over. I wonder how many have sold." Wrapping my arms around her shoulders, I plant a kiss on her neck and whisper, "Have I told you how proud of you I am?"

With a sigh, Hailee leans into my touch. "I'm proud of you too."

"Me? I haven't done anything."

"I believe it's your face plastered all around this room. If people are buying, it's not just me they're investing in, it's you too."

Just then, Angelique spots us and waves us over. "Hailee, Aroha." Her smile stretches from ear to ear, and I notice her face is glowing. "I've just heard the best news!" She takes a breath before blurting out, "They're all gone!"

"What?"

"The paintings, they're all sold!"

"Are you serious?" Hailee grabs for my hand to steady herself. "All of them?"

"Every single one has been bought. Isn't that fantastic?" She beams, her eyes sparkling with delight.

"Congratulations." A meaty hand extends towards us, and I realise it belongs to the stocky guy I saw talking to Angelique.

"Uh, thanks."

"Oh! Where are my manners? This is Ethan. He's one of the Nomads." Her cheeks flush as she strokes a hand down his arm. "This is Hailee and Aroha."

"Nice to meet you."

"You too. This is some party." He nods his head, looking around the room, completely at ease.

"How do you two know each other?" I enquire, a smile playing across my face.

"Oh, we don't. Not really. We just met." Angelique brushes a stray hair behind her ear, shifting from one foot to another like a nervous school girl.

"She's a gorgeous woman. Can't blame a guy for trying." He winks, lifting his glass to his lips.

"Oh." She waves a hand through the air dismissively, but I can tell she's flattered. It seems this man has gotten under her skin.

Chapter Ten

Dan

Cara is splayed out in front of me, her legs still hooked over my shoulders, while Bri sits to the side looking all demure, and not at all like she's just taken part in a sordid ménage trois. Her cheeks are flushed as she stares at Cara, waiting for her to tell me what the hell is going on. When I'd first seen them here at my Christmas work do, I'd thought it was a happy coincidence, but now I feel like it was all some elaborate plan to get me here, buck naked. I don't know whether to be turned on or scared shitless.

As the silence draws on, a thought occurs to me. My eyes scan the room for cameras or anything that could incriminate me. Just last month one of my old crew was done for lude conduct in a public place and benched for the finals. *God, how could I be so stupid?*

"How much?" I drop Cara's legs from my grasp and get to my feet, searching for my pants. *Where the hell did she throw them?*

"How much what?" Bri asks, her head snapping to face me.

"Wow. Really? You think we're trying to blackmail you?" Cara pushes up to her elbows, a fire in her eyes. Bri flings an arm across her bare chest, looking as though she might cry.

"I knew this was a bad idea. We should have just told him as soon as we saw him."

"Told me what?"

Cara's eyes soften as she turns to Bri, cupping her face and bringing their foreheads together. "Everything will be fine, with or without him."

"With or without me? Can someone please explain what's going on?" Swiping my pants off a canary-yellow bike in the corner, I quickly pull them on.

Cara stands, pulling her dress back up over her curves before speaking. "Well, Danny boy, it seems our little romp between the sheets gave us more than we bargained for."

"More than we bargained for? What the hell does that even mean?"

She places a hand on her stomach, raising an eyebrow, and my throat goes dry as I take in her meaning.

"It means there's going to be a little Carbridan in seven months' time." She turns to Bri with a scrunched nose. "We might need to work on the name."

"Wait," I stutter. "You're… We're…" I wave a finger between the three of us. "We're having a baby?"

"Technically, *I'm* having the baby, but yeah, you're the baby daddy." She waves her hands in the air. "Surprise!"

Bri steps up behind Cara, peering over her shoulder. "Are you mad?"

"Am I...?" I rake a hand through my hair, trying to wrap my head around this news. "I'm going to be a dad?"

"That's kinda how it works, yeah." Cara rolls her eyes. "Didn't your folks teach you about the birds and the bees? Geez."

I pace the floor between the cheddar moon and the canary bike. "I'm going to be a dad." A smile pulls at the corner of my lips. "I'm going to be a dad?" Bri nods, her teeth worrying her bottom lip as she waits out my reaction. My head is reeling, but my heart is about ready to burst with pride. Spinning around, I rush at them, picking Cara up and swinging her around the room before planting a kiss on Bri's cheek. "I'm going to be a dad!"

Chapter Eleven

Cara

Bri stops short, her hand clutching at my arm. "Are you seeing what I'm seeing?"

Following her gaze, I let out a holler, "Hallelujah! It's a Christmas miracle!" Ethan is in the corner with a tall, wispy-haired woman, playing tonsil hockey. Finally!

"Aww." Bri claps her hands. "Ethan's got himself a girl, we've got ourselves a baby. This is looking to be a Christmas to remember."

"That's for sure." Dan slings an arm around each of us. "So, how're we going to do this? You moving in, Cara? Or are we finding a new place together?"

"Um, hold up." I spin to face him. "Are we making this a thing now? Like a throuple?"

A crease forms on Dan's brow. "Uh, yeah, how else were you going to do it?"

"I was thinking something like *My Two Dad's* only it'd be me and Bri with a baby daddy on the side. Ya know, like a cash cow."

His jaw drops, his eyes flicking between us both before he grins. "You're fucking with me, aren't you?"

"When am I *not* fucking with you, Danny boy?" I look to Bri.

Her eyes sparkle as she nods, pulling her lip between her teeth. "I'm game if you are."

"Well then, I guess it's official. Bridancar are going it throuple styles."

Bri laughs, looping her arm through mine and Dan's. "We really need to work on those names."

Acknowledgements

I have to thank Kat T Masen for suggesting someone host a Christmas signing, which in turn made me decide to turn Wham Bam Author Jam into a Christmas themed signing, which then meant I needed to write a novella to go with it! *A Gift to Remember* wasn't even a blip on my radar, but I feel like it's given the characters of the pocket rocket novellas thus far, a nice little end to their stories.

I always have to thank Trina for going over my words with a fine-toothed comb. I trust you not to let me do anything stupid!

Thanks to Nicole for being my sounding board and the one I go to when I'm stuck.

Thanks to Launa for keeping the Ink Slinging Sisters going whenever I'm stuck in the writing cave and can't interact. And of course, to the Slingers themselves, for always rallying around me and showing unwavering support. You guys rock!

And of course, to the readers, without whom I could not do what I do. From the bottom of my heart, I thank you xxx

Cyan Tayse is the pen name of a multi-genre author based in New Zealand. After a lot of coaxing from friends, she decided to embark on a journey of discovery. Yes, that's right, she embraced her desire to write things a little different to her usual, thus the Pocket Rocket and Brief Encounters novellas were born.

Cyan can often be found lurking on social media, and she loves to hear from fellow authors and readers.